ONE KISS

A SHORT STORY FROM THE BECAUSE BEARDS ANTHOLOGY

MARTHA SWEENEY

ONE KISS: A SHORT STORY

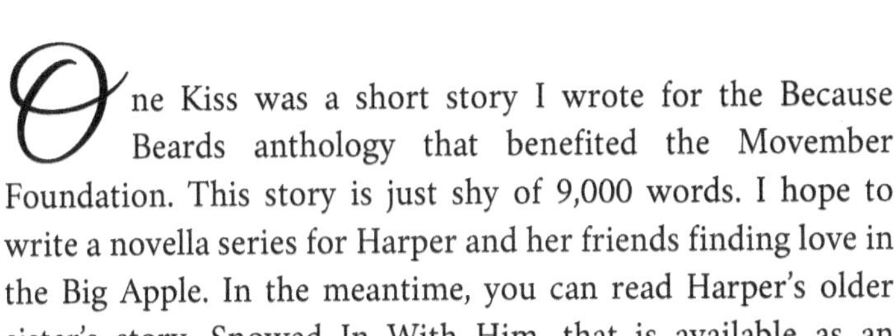

One Kiss was a short story I wrote for the Because Beards anthology that benefited the Movember Foundation. This story is just shy of 9,000 words. I hope to write a novella series for Harper and her friends finding love in the Big Apple. In the meantime, you can read Harper's older sister's story, Snowed In With Him, that is available as an ebook on all retailers and as a paperback via my website.

HARPER

"**S**top sulking, Harper," Adele says for the sixth time tonight.

"I'm not sulking," I challenge with a dramatic pouty face.

"Yes, you are," supports Ayris with an unamused and unaffected expression.

"No, I'm not," I lie as I mock whine and drag out my words. I lose composure and a smile cracks slightly on my face.

"It's New Year's Eve," Brooke states the obvious. "It's going to be a new year, therefore, a new *you*."

"I don't want a new me," I say, continuing to fake fuss.

"You just need a new attitude," Adele corrects, throwing some sass my way with a smack to my hip.

"My attitude is just fine," I reply, sticking my tongue out at her.

"Not since you dumped Owen's ass two weeks before Christmas," Ayris reminds with a snicker followed by her own tongue's appearance.

My smile lowers slightly in a moment of defeat, but I swallow the pain quickly, causing the very pain the girls are talking about to surface a little as I try to brush it away. "Fuck off."

"Someone needs to get laid," Brooke quips.

"No," I counter. "I just need my heart removed."

"Owen is a loser," Adele announces. "He didn't deserve you."

"We told you he was a player," Ayris comments.

"No, you didn't," I deny.

"Well, in a roundabout way we did," Adele defends.

"On several occasions," Brooke adds. "You just didn't want to listen."

"It's not our fault that you were blinded by hot sex, hot abs, hot arms, and that smile," Ayris states followed by a sigh as she looks off into the distance as if picturing Owen's glorious body. She catches herself quickly, righting her expression and tone. "And, it's not our fault that you didn't want to see that he was sleeping around until you caught him," Ayris states.

The fucker was screwing some chick on my couch — my couch!

"At least he asked if you wanted to join them," Ayris reminds.

"After the fact," I say heatedly.

"Fucking models," Brooke huffs.

"Fucking men," Adele proclaims.

This gets a smile from me. My girlfriends always know how to cheer me up. We know how to raise each other's spirits when the time comes. There's the initial sad and depressed phase that includes a lot of tissues, takeout food, and junk food that is filled with understanding and compassion. Then, there's the anger phase where we hate all men and where I workout my frustration in the gym on a punching bag, which is then quickly followed by the love of men as soon as we spot a sexy one with a great ass and smile — which then eventually leads us right back to the beginning of the cycle.

"You know what you need, Harper?" Ayris asks.

"What?" I reply nervously.

"A one-night stand," she returns.

"No," I object. "I don't need any man in my pants right now unless he's battery-operated."

"How about your mouth?" Adele snickers.

"What?" I reply, choking on the sip of my sour apple martini.

"You do need someone to smooch with when the clock strikes twelve."

"I don't think that's a good idea," I counter.

"It's a *great* idea!" shouts Brooke.

"Making out with a stranger on New Year's is the best way to get over a guy," Adele confirms.

"Uh…no," I counter.

"Uh…yeah," Ayris interjects. "It helped me two years ago and Brooke the year before that.

"It definitely helped," encourages Brooke. "Especially if one of us takes a picture of it and then sends it to Owen."

"No," I reply as my eyes inflate a little. I pause for a second, considering the option. I wouldn't mind having a picture of me making out with a hot guy sent to Owen. It would show him that I've moved on and that he's missing out.

"I've got an idea," Ayris announces. "He's got to be *not* your usual type."

"What?" I laugh nervously.

"Yes!" Adele shouts supportively.

"No," I challenge, though I'm kind of excited by the idea.

"Shut up. It's happening," Ayris directs.

I smile to myself as the idea settles in.

"No pretty boys," Brooke begins plotting.

"And, no average ones," Ayris adds. "They don't have as much stamina or experience as the ones with a good body."

"We can't have our girl hooking up with a guy who hasn't

had enough experience kissing, let alone look any less attractive than Owen," Adele adds.

"He's got to be hotter and sexier than Owen," Brooke comments.

My mouth opens to comment, but they keep shooting off ideas and at least one or two of them are talking at the same time, not giving me a second to be heard even if I did jump in. My eyes dart back and forth between them as I watch diarrhea of the mouth flow freely around me.

"Tall. He's got to be tall," Adele says.

"She always goes for guys who are eye level when she's wearing heels and she won't wear anything taller than three inches," Ayris claims.

"So, he'll have to be over six foot," Brooke says.

"His eyes," Ayris adds. "They have to be dreamy...and sparkle."

"Yes," agrees Adele.

"Dark and brooding with a hint of softness," Brooke includes.

"What color?" Adele asks.

"Doesn't matter," Ayris returns. "It'll depend on the gaze and feeling he gives off."

"What about his clothes?" Adele asks. "He can't be too nice or preppy looking."

"Or sloppy," Brooke mentions.

"I would say that depends on his face," Ayris returns. "Ooh....he needs to be scruffy or have a beard."

"No!" I interject, but they ignore me.

I hate, no, I loathe beards, especially the ones that just grow and aren't well taken care of. It's a pet peeve of mine.

"Yes!" the three of them shout at the same time.

"You hate beards," Ayris reminds. "So, a beard is a must!"

"Fuck me," I mumble, knowing that they're not going to

stop until they pick a guy, and even worse until I actually kiss him tonight.

"Okay…so, I think we have our description of him," Adele states.

"A badass vibe, but with sweet, intense eyes, at least week-old facial hair, or more, but it has to be well trimmed, 'cause you ladies know how if he's not willing to keep his face looking nice, then the rest of him is icky…tall, handsome and rugged at the same time…definitely *tats* if we can see them above the collar or on his arms with the sleeves rolled up." Ayris summaries.

"No," I object.

"You don't have a say in this," Adele challenges.

"If my lips are connecting with his, I do," I argue.

"Nope," Brooke interjects. "You lost the ability to weigh in on this."

"Since when?" I huff.

"Since you had a bad judgment call on the last two guys you dated," Adele comments.

"Now, ladies," Ayris states excitedly. "Let's see who we can find."

They stand up at the same time from our booth and I watch the three of them scan the party and cringe at the very idea of all of this. A dreadfully nervous feeling stirs in my belly, causing me to stand in hopes of seeing who I'm going to be paired with just in case I'm going to have to drink more for it to happen.

"There!" Adele shouts, pointing in a direction.

I shift to see where they're looking as they whisper to each other, but they're blocking my view. The three of them quickly turn around and sit before I can see who they've chosen from the blob of bodies.

"Who?" I inquire, plopping down in my seat again.

"We'll tell you…." Brooke snickers.

My head tilts in a request for her to expound, but she doesn't.

"We'll tell you…but when it gets closer to midnight. That way you don't try to run and hide," Ayris replies with a devious grin.

"Here," Brooke says, handing me her drink. "You're going to need some liquid courage."

"No," I refuse. "I don't want to be hammered."

"You need to have a good enough buzz if you're going to do it," Ayris states.

"Fine," I huff, taking Brooke's martini and chugging the rest of it.

"Ten minutes," Adele announces after checking her phone. "Let's take our positions for who we're going to kiss."

"I'll keep an eye on this one," Ayris announces. Her head tilts in my direction.

"What?" I question with mock hurt feelings.

"You can't be trusted," Ayris says. "So, I'll pick one of his friends to kiss."

"You all suck," I announce.

"We know," Adele confirms happily.

"I've been told I *suck* really well," Ayris quips.

The four of us giggle and then chug the last of our drinks before getting up in search of our grand finale for the night.

2

REESE

The guys drag me out for New Year's, knowing that I'm not in the mood to party, let alone be with a bunch of rowdy strangers. Do I like to have a good time? Yes. It's just that I'm on-call for work and can't really relax. I'd much rather be at my place or one of theirs hanging out with a few friends, playing video games, pool, or anything other than being at this club with over four hundred people in it. We're crammed in and you can barely move two feet without bumping into several people at the same time, let alone the loud music and flashing lights that are making it hard to see.

Any other night, when I can actually relax and cut loose, I'm always up for getting out of the apartment. The guys keep me sane when it comes to being social and I don't mind chatting, having a few beers, and checking out the hot women in the bars and clubs we frequent each month. Tonight, however, I have to be a bit more reserved with my choices of drinks and who I'm willing to socialize with other than my friends.

I got used to working so much at the last hospital I was employed at that I had forgotten what it was like to have friends, let alone a social life, until I moved back here to New

York eight months ago. My last job was too stressful. There should have been at least three more doctors on payroll, but the manager was cheap and an ass. He'd have us work twenty-hour shifts if he could, especially us younger, newer vets. I started working there while I was in college and stayed on once I graduated. When work consumed my life to the point where I wasn't even getting the chance to visit any family during holidays for an entire year, I quit and came back home. I had enough money saved up to afford to move in with the guys and look for a job for at least a year. With my excellent grades and the fact that I had worked at the same place for as long as I did, the first place I interviewed with hired me. Overall, the hours are better and the pay is much more.

"Come on, man," Gabe encourages. "Relax at least a little." He hands me a beer.

"I can't," I counter.

"It's almost midnight," Logan states. "Don't be a pussy and at least have *a* drink."

"I am what I eat," I reply with a grin, wanting to redirect our conversation off of me.

I've been with a few kind-of-serious girlfriends and none of them have complained about my *bikini burger-munching* ability as Gabe calls it. I snort to myself at the phrase.

"Nice," Carter laughs, high-fiving me.

"Drink it slowly," Gabe states. "You're not going to find a chick to kiss if you don't have a drink in your hand."

"A drink doesn't sway a woman to kiss a guy or not," I argue.

"At a place like this, it does," Gabe replies. "I've already got three potential chicks."

"How?" I investigate.

Gabe always has fucked up logic when it comes to dating and the opposite sex.

"'Cause I got skills, man," Gabe boasts.

"You wish," Logan interjects. "Remember last weekend?"

Logan, Carter, and I laugh at the memory. A chick walked out of Gabe's bedroom, complaining about how he was unable to *eat her peach* properly after trying for about thirty minutes.

"That's bullshit," Gabe challenges. "And, as I said, she did *not* have a peach. It was more like a shag carpet. I mean…come on ladies. Wax that shit!"

"And…that's why you have a challenge with the ladies," Carter roasts.

"No, I don't," Gabe argues.

I take a sip of the beer Gabe gave me, chuckling at their banter as I scan the room. It's been three months since I've been in a relationship and I'm missing the benefits of one. The last chick I dated, Lily, was interesting. I'm not one to bash women, but she was a pain in the ass when she was trying to change me just two months into us seeing each other; this while she was apparently fucking two other guys and also blatantly tried hooking up with Gabe too. So, I dumped her that night and never looked back.

As the night ticks on, I nurse my beer and shoot the shit with my friends when they aren't talking with a chick. A number of drunk ones, really drunk ones, come up to us, but I don't pay them much attention. Yeah, they're cute, but I'm not into the slutty-drunkard chicks who are as obvious as the ones that I'm seeing tonight. I'm all about having a good time, but to get yourself that inebriated is not my thing.

At some point, I check my phone for the time and notice that it's almost midnight. For starters, I'm double-checking to make sure I didn't miss a call alerting me that the hospital needs me as well as to find out how much longer until I can head home and get some sleep since I have the morning shift.

Suddenly, someone bumps into me.

"Sorry," a female voice says.

I look down and am met with sparkling, amber eyes that

are surrounded by golden, long hair. My eyes immediately drop to her lips and I feel my caveman instincts kicking in. I lose my breath when she smiles. My dick hardens instantly and my throat dries, forcing me to chug the rest of my beer.

"Ayris, back up," she shouts, pushing her friend off of her.

The friend looks drunk, but I'm not sure about the goddess before me. Her mouth moves again when she looks back at me, but I can't make out her words.

"What?" I ask, leaning forward to hear her.

"Sorry," she repeats, leaning the rest of the way into me.

Her warm, plump breasts press into my chest and it feels like I'm about to come in my pants. Man, does she smell fucking amazing.

"My friend gets a little excited at New Year's," she states as her lips brush against my earlobe two times as she speaks.

Instinctually, my free hand darts to her hip, holding her steady when her friend and two others bump into her, pushing her further into my body.

We exchange a nervous smile when she pulls her face away from my chest. Our eyes stay locked and it's as if all the commotion around us dissolves. Time stands still at this very moment as I stare at her lips. Now I know who I'm going to kiss tonight.

Without warning, her mouth is on mine. When she pulls away for a breath, my hand moves quickly from her hip to her back, capturing her neck and pulling her closer. My tongue darts out, eager to taste more of the candy flavor of her lips. She returns the embrace, snaking one of her hands up my chest, behind my neck, and into my hair. Her tongue tastes just as sweet as her lips and my dick gets even harder at the thought of her pussy having the same flavor.

"See," Logan's voice says in my ear. "We told you there'd be a chick to kiss."

My eyes dart around, wondering where she has suddenly gone.

"You okay, man?" Logan asks.

"Where did she go?" I search feeling dazed and confused.

"Who?"

"The chick I was just kissing," I state.

"Don't know," Logan replies. "I just saw the back of her head. The first time just before you two kissed and then again right before her friend kissed me after I just kissed some other chick."

"Fuck," I groan.

"Do you think they'd be up for a three-way?" Logan inquires.

Ignoring him, I look frantically for the goddess who blessed me with the taste of heaven. I dart through the crowd that seems still caught up in the rush of the new year arriving, desperate to find her, but my Cinderella is nowhere to be found.

3

HARPER

$\mathcal{I}$t's been four weeks since New Year's Eve and I can honestly say that I feel great and that Owen has barely crossed my mind. The girls keep saying that it's all because of the kiss I had with Mr. tall, grey-eyed, sexy beard, at least one partially hidden forearm tattoo, dreamy hunk. I don't agree with them one hundred percent, but that was the best fucking kiss I've ever had in my whole life.

I'm no slut, but I've kissed a lot of boys since I was fourteen. I'd have to say I've made out with at least twelve, maybe more during my drunken bouts in college, but have only slept with five of them. I'm a firm believer in a girl getting to know her body as well as her own wants, desires, and fantasies before getting married.

That kiss replays in my mind several times a day and especially when I masturbate. He smelled divine, his lips were so soft yet firm enough to know how to kiss, his tongue was tasty and I actually enjoyed the scratch of his scruff against my skin. I found myself gliding my fingers along his chin twice as we made out for some strange reason. I hate the look of beards, but his was mesmerizing. He looked rugged and sexy and I

17

loved the way it tickled my lips and cheeks. I walked away from that kiss reluctantly, but I'm glad I left when I did. My chest was pulsing. I was panting, and I felt like if we kept going that I was going to do more than just make out with the guy.

Part of me wonders if I'll ever see him again. I chide myself at night when masturbation only goes so far for not at least sticking around to see what would have happened with him. I've had a one-night stand before. It didn't go well, mind you, but for some reason, this guy seemed like he would have been more than just one night.

Today, I head out about a half hour before the sun is scheduled to rise. The girls can sleep through almost anything, so I don't have to walk around the apartment like a cat. The four of us live together in New York to keep our rent and other expenses low, live safely, and somehow save money when we're not spending it on clothes, shoes, books, food, and wine.

Brooke's a nurse, Adele is a bartender, Ayris works for a fashion magazine, and I'm a photographer slash graphic designer. I work mostly from home, running my own online business. I do a wide range of photography, trying to always keep myself open to new opportunities and to keep it interesting. Ayris' magazine has used me for a few spreads, mostly last-minute photo shoots where something happened. I never asked what occurred exactly for them to need me in just a few hour's notice, but I was grateful for the money, the exposure, and what it did for my portfolio. My shots have never been on the front cover, but I've at least had those as a part of my resume if I ever need them. I've started a collection of each magazine I'm in aside from a general portfolio online.

Mondays are my favorite day when everyone else in New York hates them. While people are late getting up to head to work for the day, I'm already finishing up either a workout class, a jog, or a long walk (paired with the occasional ride on the subway) through the different streets of New York, taking photos of anything that inspires me.

Today's trip is with a hot chocolate through Central Park and my camera in hand, enjoying the hazy, cool morning as most avoid the outdoors during this time of year. On my way back to the apartment, I grab another cup of hot chocolate and relax in the cafe's window box that overlooks the street. I read a little when I'm not peering out the window people-watching.

After hanging at the cafe for at least twenty minutes, I make my way home. The cool nip in the air doesn't bother me too much since my body is warm from the hot liquid I just had, so I lazily make my way down an extra few blocks to the next subway station. The platform is a bit crowded, but I'm able to get through pretty easily. With my camera already packed, I reach into my bag and grab my book to start reading.

Once the train arrives, my eyes stay on the page as I use my peripheral to maneuver through the people getting on and off of the train. I don't bother taking a seat, knowing most people need it more than I do. With my left arm wrapped around the pole to steady myself for when the train disembarks, I keep my nose in my book.

"Hey," a male voice shouts.

Normally, I don't bother reacting to people on the subway, but for some strange reason, my gaze lifts. My mouth gapes in astonishment as I see him; the hunk I kissed at New Year's. The doors begin to close as he tries to get close enough to get on. It's as if time stands still for everything except the doors. Our eyes stay locked as the train begins to move. Neither of us says anything as he tries to follow the train. His gorgeous eyes suddenly vanish from my view and my head jerks to the left, wishing they could see more of him.

4

REESE

I can't believe I fucking saw her. I was starting to wonder if I'd ever see my Cinderella again. I was instantly jealous of her teeth, having her sexy lips captured between them. Blood drained quickly to my groin, giving me an instant boner and temporarily slowing me down as I tried to get back onto the train. My legs couldn't move fast enough to get to her, and when the doors closed, I was devastated.

Every day since our second encounter, which was three weeks ago, I've gone to that station at the exact same time, unless the trains are running late, hoping to see her. I don't know if she was leaving for work or just getting home from it. It doesn't really matter, I just need to find her.

She consumes my thoughts and dreams. I'm a guy, so yeah, my carnal urges crave her. I want nothing else but to be buried inside her. I masturbate before going to bed, dreaming that it's her, and wake up with a raging hard-on that needs my fantasy to become reality.

Once I satisfy my physical needs, my mind races to discover her name, favorite color, favorite thing to eat, was the book she was reading for school or pleasure and so much more.

"Dr. Langford?"

"Hm?" I reply as my eyes flit across the iPad while I struggle to finish making notes.

"Dr. Langford," she repeats.

"Yes. Sorry, Mrs. Hildreth," I reply.

"Puppy love," she states.

"What?" I ask.

"It's in your eyes," Mrs. Hildreth informs. "What's her name?"

"I…I don't know," I answer truthfully.

"What do you mean you don't know?"

"It's complicated," I sigh.

"Love is complicated," she declares.

"We only met twice," I inform. "I'd hardly call it love."

"You're young, so I know you don't recognize it as such," she presents. "But, it is definitely love…regardless of whether you know her name or not. Soulmates from past lives who are working to find each other again."

"Sure," I comment, brushing it off.

"So…tell me about her as you examine Charlie," she encourages.

"There's nothing really to tell," I lie, shifting on my feet.

"Come on," Mrs. Hildreth coaxes.

"Besides, it's not professional for me to divulge personal information with patients," I remind.

"I'm not a patient," Mrs. Hildreth counters.

"You know what I mean," I state with a smile.

"Charlie doesn't mind…do you, Charlie?" she asks.

Charlie meows and then brushes his head up against my arm.

"Hello, Charlie," I greet, petting him. "How are you today?"

"He's good," Mrs. Hildreth informs. "I think he got one of the neighbor's cats pregnant."

"Pregnant?" I repeat. "He's fixed."

"That's what I thought," Mrs. Hildreth laughs. "Looks like the surgery didn't take."

"Did Dr. Manning do the procedure?" I inspect.

"No," she confirms. "When I adopted him they said on his paperwork that he was fixed."

"Well, we need to check…and if he's not, would you like us to schedule it?" I check.

"Yes," Mrs. Hildreth replies. "I don't need any more baby mamas getting mad at me and Charlie here."

I snicker at the phrase *baby mamas* coming out of Mrs. Hildreth's mouth since she's in her sixties or seventies.

"You'll find her," Mrs. Hildreth announces.

"Who?"

"Your lady friend," she clarifies. "Love never fails."

I smile and nod, hoping she's right.

5

HARPER

*I*t's been six weeks since I saw him at the train station. When I can, I veer from some of my daily routine and visit that stop, hoping to bump into him again. I still take a different route heading out for my morning workout class, jog, or photography journeys, but always make sure that when I go home, I take the same train at the exact same station as close to the same time as possible. I don't get to hang around the station because of what happened the fourth time I did. A few guys tried to mess with me, but when I threatened to use the mace I have on my keychain and lied about being a black belt, they backed off. I'm not so sure it was the mace, my threat, or as much as it was the homeless man that came to my so-called rescue. Though he smelled, he wasn't weird and didn't try to bother me after coming to my aid. So since then, I've gotten to know him a little more each time I'm there.

The first five times I saw the homeless man, he was just sitting on a bench in the back, minding his own business. He never begged for money and didn't have a cup out or anything like that. I know I'm not supposed to talk to strangers, but to me, he doesn't seem like one since he stood up for me.

"Hey, Allen," I greet, sitting down next to him.

"Hey, Harper," he returns with a smile.

"I brought you something," I say, extending my right hand.

"You shouldn't have," he replies, taking the lemonade and bag that has a sandwich and danish. "But, thank you."

I usually get him a black coffee, his favorite, but decided to change it up a little since today is a little warmer than usual for the middle of a New York March.

"Don't argue with me," I tease.

"You…never," he laughs. Allen gulps down half of the lemonade. "It tastes different this time."

"It's almost spring," I remind. "So, they add lavender to it. Don't you like it?"

"No, I love it," he praises.

"Good," I giggle. "I'll make sure to get it again next time."

"Yes, please," Allen encourages, munching on his sandwich. "So, have you found him yet?"

"No," I sigh.

"Part of me wants you to find him," Allen shares, taking a huge bite. He chews for about ten seconds and then swallows a little. "But, part of me doesn't."

"What? Why?" I ask with a laugh.

"If you find him, you'll forget all about me," Allen returns with a grinning mouthful of food.

"I could never forget you," I say with a smile.

"I know," Allen replies confidently. "So, what can you give me to identify him?"

"Why?"

"Well, I might have seen him and most likely will again. And, if I do, I can tell him something for you," Allen offers.

"Aww. You'd do that for me?" I ask, touched by his gesture.

"Of course," Allen confirms. "You take good care of me." He holds up the last bit of his sandwich.

"I don't know," I return nervously.

"What do you not know? You want to find him, right?" Allen checks.

"Yeah."

"Well, what's the problem then?" he searches.

"I kind of like the mystery behind it all," I confess.

"Clues are good for a mystery," Allen suggests.

"True," I agree.

"So?" Allen checks after about a minute.

"So, I don't know," I say.

"Worried that the reality isn't as grand as the fantasy?" Allen asks.

"Kind of," I sigh.

"You women make it more complicated than it needs to be," he states.

"Complicated can be fun," I return with a devious smile.

"Yes. But, it can also be a pain in the ass," Allen goads.

"True," I reply.

6

REESE

’m starting to lose hope. It's been eight weeks since we saw each other at the train station. I've gone every day and haven't found her and I'm starting to think that it was just a coincidence that we ran into each other. The guys and I have even been back to the club a few times, but I haven't seen her there either.

I do my best to distract myself at work, at the gym, or with the guys, because I know it's not completely healthy that she consumes as much of my thoughts and desires. I don't notice other women unless they possibly look like my Cinderella. When I've gone up to a few of them, thinking they were her, I was instantly disappointed. The women seemed excited that I stopped them, but not so happy when I walk away without a word or explanation.

"Why are we going back to this place again?" Gabe whines.

"Because…" Carter replies. "Reese is in love."

"I'm not in love," I challenge, scratching my beard.

"Yeah, you are," Logan states. "It's okay. We know how you get."

"How do I get it?" I ask.

"You get one taste of a woman and you're hooked," Carter shares. "You don't see any other chick until things end with the one you want."

"That's not true," I counter.

"Yeah, it is," Gabe laughs. "The last two months, you haven't even made eye contact with another woman."

"Yes, I have," I argue. "I look directly at my patients and their owners."

"They don't count," Logan presents.

"Sure they do," I counter.

"I was referring to potential chicks to date or fuck," Logan reiterates.

"Whatever," I huff, despite my crumbling opposition.

"It's okay, man," Carter soothes. "We get it. It's just funny since you've only kissed her at New Year's and haven't seen her since."

"I have seen her," I mention.

"What? When?" Carter asks.

"It was about a month after the party. I had gotten off the train for work and saw her getting on," I explain. "We saw each other, but I haven't seen her since."

"Why didn't you tell us?" Logan asks.

"Because you'd make fun of me," I inform.

"No, we wouldn't," Carter replies.

"I would," Gabe states.

"We know you would," Logan replies. "But you weren't included in the *we*."

"Why don't you put out flyers around the station?" Gabe teases. "I'm sure she'd see them and would contact you."

"Ass," I hiss.

"It kind of makes sense," Logan defends.

"Maybe you could talk to one of the station workers," Carter suggests. "Is there anyone who's regularly there each time you get off from work?"

"You said *get off*," Gabe laughs.

"Mature," I reply unimpressed.

Normally, I would laugh at Gabe's vulgarity, but not today. I'm too stressed out with not being able to find Cinderella.

"There are thousands of people that go through that station each morning," I remind. "There's no way in hell a worker would remember or recognize her," I comment.

"You never know," Logan returns. "She could be friends with someone there."

"What are the odds of that?" I quip.

"Probably slim," Carter says. "But, anything is possible... even if the odds are slim in your favor."

"Thanks, Mr. Physics," I tease.

"Happy to help keep your hopes up," Carter replies with a grin.

"What's her name?" Logan asks.

"Don't know," I return.

"You didn't get it on New Year's?" Logan checks.

"Nope," I confirm. "We were too busy kissing...and then, she was suddenly gone."

"Man's on a mission," Carter comments.

"I'm on a mission," Gabe interjects. "On a mission to get laid."

"Shocking," Carter replies.

"Don't hate the player," Gabe states. "Just hate the game."

"You aren't a player," Logan jabs. "You're on the sidelines most of the time by your own default."

"Am not," Gabe argues. "You boys are on the sidelines. You've put yourselves there...especially you, Reese."

I roll my eyes even though Gabe is right.

"What?" Gabe asks. "It's true. You could have been getting some all this time while you look for her. It's not like you two were or are dating."

"He does have a point," Carter supports.

"I bet she's already forgotten about you," Gabe adds.

"Don't be a dick," Carter says. "Just because you've been having trouble getting some."

"I haven't had trouble," Gabe shouts, walking away.

Logan, Carter, and I look back and forth at each other for a few beats, smiling at the jab.

"Well, I'm sure you'll find her again," Logan encourages.

"That's what Mrs. Hildreth says," I share.

"Who?" Logan checks.

"One of the patient's owners from the hospital," I reply.

"You saw her a second time," Carter reminds. "So, the odds are definitely more in your favor that you actually see her again."

7

HARPER

"**H**arper," Ayris hollers from outside the room.

"What?" I reply as I get out of the shower.

"I have an emergency meeting at the office," she shares, barging into the bathroom.

This is typical behavior for all of the girls in the apartment, so her seeing me naked is nothing new.

"So?" I say, grabbing my towel and wrapping it around me.

"So, I will love you forever if you can do me a huge favor," Ayris states.

"What do you need?" I ask, getting a second towel for my hair.

"Mr. Darcy is supposed to have his checkup today and I really don't want to cancel," she informs.

"Why not?" I ask. "It's not like you haven't rescheduled before."

"I know," she sighs, grabbing the deodorant and handing it to me when I reach for it.

"Then?" I coax.

"I called," Ayris explains. "The problem is that they're booked solid for the next three months."

"So?"

"So, with the way that his insurance is, it can't wait three months," Ayris replies. "Besides, it's not like you have anything to do."

"Ouch," I reply with a pout.

"Oh, stop it," she directs. "You know what I mean."

"Do I?" I goad playfully.

"Come on," Ayris whines. "You know I love you. It's just that you've got more flexibility than the rest of us since you work from home."

"So, you do admit that I work?" I check with a grin.

"Yes," she huffs. "I acknowledge that you do work, making a good living from the comfort of our couch…which I'm jealous of…but I need your help for this."

"You're not jealous," I tease. "You love the drama that comes with your job."

"True," she confirms. "But, I really don't want to have to be paying out of pocket for the appointment if I don't have to."

"Got your eye on some new shoes?" I goad.

"No," she returns.

I study her for a second to see if she's telling the truth. "What time is the appointment?" I check.

"Ten-thirty," she replies.

"What time is it now?" I ask.

"It's only eight-thirty," she states, looking at her phone. "Shit, I'm already late."

"Sure," I agree. "I've got plenty of time to finish getting ready."

"Great!" she shouts. "I love you." Ayris wraps her arms around my shoulders.

"Love you too," I reply, patting her arm. "Now, get out of my way so I can finish getting ready."

"You're the best," she says, darting out of the bathroom.

"And, you're running late," I tease.

"Shit!" Ayris exclaims. There's commotion somewhere in the apartment. "See you later," Ayris says with her voice sounding more distant.

"See you later," I yell.

Mr. Darcy hangs out with me in my room as I get dressed. Ayris got him about a month after the four of us started living together in this apartment three years ago. We had just graduated college and we have been practically inseparable since unless we're at work or naked with a man.

Mr. Darcy has a sweet temperament, acting more like a dog sometimes than an actual cat. He loves to snuggle, be petted, and play most of the time he's awake. He's definitely spoiled by the four of us, but he doesn't seem to mind.

When it comes time to leave, Mr. Darcy happily climbs inside his crate. He's never really minded it and likes to hide in it some days. The two of us make our way down to the station just two blocks from our building, only having to wait for the train for about three minutes. A few children seem interested when they see the crate, peering in from a distance.

Ten minutes later, I exit the train and stop over to see Allen.

"Hey, cutie," Allen greets when I'm a few feet away.

"Hey, yourself," I reply with a smile.

"Who's your friend?" Allen asks.

I look around me. "There's no one with me silly," I tease.

"I meant the fur ball in the cage," Allen corrects, pointing to Mr. Darcy.

"Oh," I giggle. "This is Mr. Darcy. My roommate's cat."

"Hello, Mr. Darcy," Allen greets, placing his finger against the gate.

Mr. Darcy wraps his paw around Allen's finger.

"Looks like he likes me," Allen chuckles.

"Yeah," I encourage. "He's pretty friendly."

"Where you two headed?" Allen asks.

"Mr. Darcy has a checkup," I inform. "After that, we'll be having lunch."

"Wonderful," Allen praises.

"Do you want your usual?" I check.

"You're too good to me," Allen states.

"I'll take that as a yes," I return with a smile. "We should be back in about an hour or two. Can you wait that long?"

"I'll wait for you as long as I need to, cutie," Allen professes.

"Don't tease me," I challenge.

"Me? Never," Allen returns with a wicked smile.

"I'm still job hunting for you," I inform. "I wish I was more successful to be able to hire you."

"You buying me lunch most days is more than enough," Allen says.

"Behave," I tease.

"Never," he laughs as I walk away to get onto the train.

Mr. Darcy and I get to the vet's office about ten minutes early. As we wait, I see that there is a sign looking for someone who can help with the night shift watch for the animals and I instantly think of Allen. I inquire to the woman at the desk and she happily gives me some information and answers my questions about the position. Looks like today is going to be an even better day.

"**D**r. Langford," one of the nurses calls as I inspect a chart outside of a room.

"Yes," I reply, keeping my eyes down on the iPad I'm using to call up patient files.

"Fifi is in room three," she informs me.

"Great," I return.

"Her owner has been here for about twenty minutes already," the nurse states. "Might want to get to her first since she's a little concerned with the pregnancy."

"Thank you," I reply.

I finish making notes, hit save, and then call up Fifi's information after clicking the schedule listed on the calendar. I review the files and the recent notes that were typed in from the call Mrs. Donahue made this morning for her appointment. The office, where I've been working for the past six months, has always been busy. There's never a dull moment. We do leave slots open for emergencies, but our time is usually limited with them since we're always so busy. The practice actually needs to hire at least another doctor to handle the constant flux of patients coming in and out daily aside from a few other staff members. They are interviewing, but from the looks of it, no one is promising yet.

After checking Fifi's vitals and noticing that her eyes lack moisture and her mouth, gums, and nose feel a bit dry, I give her water, a lot of water, and wait to run a quick urine test. From what Mrs. Donahue has told me, and from the looks of Fifi's symptoms, Fifi appears to be a little dehydrated. While waiting for the test results, I direct one of the nurses to let me know as soon as the test is complete. I use the restroom quickly before heading to the next patient.

"So, Ms. Reagan," I greet, keeping my eyes fixed on the iPad I'm holding as I open and close the door. "How's Mr. Darcy doing today?"

The only sound I hear is a cat meow followed by a faint purr after a few seconds of silence.

When I don't get a reply, I look up. "Ms. Reag...." I pause, awestruck by the sight in front of me.

I'm not sure what happens next, but the sound of the door opening paired with the nurse calling my name snaps me back to the present.

"I'm sorry, Dr. Langford," she apologizes. "I didn't mean to interrupt you...."

I turn to look at nurse Hannigan. "It's okay. What is it?"

"Fifi's results are negative," she informs me.

"That was quick," I reply. "Great. Thank you."

"You're welcome," nurse Hannigan says. After a short pause, she adds, "Would you like me to tell Fifi's owner that you'll be a minute?"

"Yes. Please let Mrs. Donahue know that I'll be right in."

"Sure thing, doctor," nurse Hannigan confirms and then leaves the room, closing the door behind her.

I turn sharply to find my Cinderella staring at me. Her eyes are wide and her mouth is still hanging open. "I'll be right back. Please, stay right here?" I instruct rather than request.

She nods slightly.

I rush out the door, quickly closing it behind me. Before I move away, I ask nurse Hannigan to make sure that no one leaves room five. She offers a small, but odd smile and nods her understanding. There's no way in hell I'm going to allow this woman to walk out of my life again.

Time seems to tick by exhaustingly slow as I inform Mrs. Donahue that Fifi is just a little dehydrated and needs to drink a little extra water. I recommend having her eat some celery or watermelon to help and which will have additional nutrients that will be beneficial to her and the puppies. It feels like it takes forever to get Mrs. Donahue to stop talking or asking me questions. She continues to speak as I escort her out of the room and down the hall to the waiting room. I appreciate the praise she's giving me in front of the other patients' owners who are waiting to be called, but this woman is tiresome and I need her to let me get back to the beauty in room five.

Standing in front of the door, I take a few deep breaths before opening it. A reassuring smile finds my face when I hear Cinderella chatting away on the other side, obviously talking to Mr. Darcy from some of the words I catch. I check my breath, run my fingers through my hair, and scratch my beard to make sure there's nothing on it from Fifi, then knock, which is quickly followed by me opening the door.

Cinderella bolts to a standing position and then adjusts her clothing and hair. The two of us stand still, not saying a single word as we hold each other's gaze.

I glance back down at the chart to catch her name so I don't sound stupid when I go to speak. I take three large steps toward her, surround her soft cheeks with my large hands and lower my lips to hers, imitating the beginning of our kiss from New Year's. She quickly returns the embrace, matching my tongue movements as her fingers return to the hair on my head once again. Her free hand cups my chin and her fingers gently rub back and forth over my beard, almost like she's petting it. I'm not sure how long we kiss, but it's long enough that both of us are panting and I'm not willing to let her go anytime soon.

"Ayris…."

"That's not my name," she interrupts.

"But, the chart says…."

"My roommate, the one who kissed your friend, is Ayris Reagan," she informs.

"Oh," I reply, clearing my throat. I suddenly feel nervous keeping her in my arms, but I'm afraid that if I let her go she'll disappear.

She offers a reassuring smile as if she just read my thoughts.

"I'm not letting you leave here until you tell me your name," I inform.

A sexy blush pops onto her cheeks, she bites her bottom lip momentarily before saying, "Harper."

"Reese," I reply. "Dr. Reese Langford."

"Nice to meet you," she replies.

"Again," I add.

Just a few seconds later and my lips are back on hers. I've got a raging hard-on that she can probably feel on her belly. We kiss for what feels like only seconds, but I know it's longer than that thanks to all of the images of things I'd like to do to her that flash through my head.

"Are…are you going to check on Mr. Darcy?" she asks after I let her mouth go for a few seconds.

"Shit," I curse under my breath.

Harper giggles.

"Once you tell me your full name," I state.

"What? Why?" she laughs nervously.

"So after today, it's that much easier to find you," I confess.

Her brows lift, but she doesn't say anything.

"I haven't stopped thinking about you since New Year's," I

admit. "And, I haven't stopped trying to find you since seeing you in the subway."

She looks down timidly for a second before her eyes return to mine. "Harper. Harper Collins."

"That's a cute name," I praise, kissing her again.

"Thanks," Harper replies in-between breaths.

"Why does that sound familiar?" I question.

A look of dread creeps onto her face.

My head tilts to the side. "As in...?"

Harper doesn't answer or ask what I'm referring to.

"As in the publishing company?" I check.

"Yes," she huffs. "My mom thought it was cute."

"I think it is," I comment, pulling her closer.

"You think that it's cute?" she asks with a shocked tone and expression.

"Yes," I confirm with a smile.

Harper shakes her head. "I don't."

"Well, I do," I return confidently, kissing her nose.

"Not," she denounces with a smirk. "It was worse when my mom actually worked for them."

"How long did she work for them?" I inquire.

Harper lets out a long sigh. "Ten years, when I was little."

"Where did she go after that?"

"Penguin gave her a better deal," she shares.

"Deal? As in she was...is an author?"

"No," Harper replies. "As in an executive editor."

"Oh," I say.

"Um...Mr. Darcy?" she reminds.

"Oh, right," I chuckle, forgetting for the second time where I am.

We gradually move apart, fixing our shirts as I grab some of the equipment needed to check the patient.

"So...how long have you been a vet?" Harper asks.

"Five years," I reply. "Who named him Mr. Darcy?"

"Ayris," she confirms.

"A fan of Pride and Prejudice, I see," I comment.

"How do you know about that?" she asks speculatively.

"I've got two older sisters," I return. "Them and my mom watch it every year in November."

Harper smiles and all I want to do is kiss her again. Strike that, I want to do more than just kiss her. Oddly, it's taking longer than usual for the blood in my dick to subside.

We're both quiet as I continue to inspect Mr. Darcy. We catch each other's gaze off and on, causing us to just smile and Harper to blush occasionally.

"Well," I say. "He's healthy."

"Good," Harper replies.

"However," I begin.

"However?" Harper asks nervously.

"However," I repeat with a smile. "I can't give him a clean bill of health until you agree to have lunch with me."

"Lunch?" she repeats.

"Yes. Lunch," I confirm. "Along with your phone number."

"Getting a little daring aren't you, doctor?" she returns with a grin.

"Yes," I confirm. "I'm known to be many things."

"Really," she giggles.

"Really," I affirm.

"On one condition," Harper states.

"Name it," I encourage.

"We go to my favorite place that's nearby," she informs.

"Done," I say quickly.

"And..." she begins, "...you seriously consider hiring my friend for the night position."

"Done," I agree. "Wait. Which friend?" I look down at the iPad. "Ayris?"

"No," Harper giggles.

"Then, who?"

"You'll meet him," she mentions.

"Him?" I ask.

"Yep."

"Him…as in a boyfriend?" I ask nervously.

"No," she replies with a giggle.

"Then, consider it done," I agree. "I've got one more patient before I'm clear to go."

"Okay."

"Will you wait for me, or am I going to have to hunt you down?" I check.

"Well…" she returns with a sexy smile. "Seeing that you know my name…even if you don't believe it is my name…you do have access to where Mr. Darcy lives, which is also where I live."

"You could be lying about living with him," I challenge playfully.

"True," she replies. "But, you do have access to my friend's home address and phone number." Her head nods slightly toward my iPad. "So, if I did run, it wouldn't be too hard to find me."

I take a few steps toward her and yank on the edge of her jacket after placing Mr. Darcy into his cage. "Just give me fifteen minutes."

"Done," she replies, sealing it with a kiss.

BONUS

On the next page, you can read the first chapter of the Barnes and Nobles BESTSELLER novel Snowed in with Him that features Harper's sister, Simone, and her journey of finding love. Snowed in with Him is a full length novel meant to be a fun, flirty, holiday read with a little bit of spice.

CHAPTER ONE - SNOWED IN WITH HIM

"Come on, Simone," Juliet whines, standing half-naked in the middle of my doorway.

"We're too old to be hanging out at bars and clubs to meet guys," I reply, not taking my eyes off my laptop.

"We're not too old for two friends to have a couple of drinks at a bar together," Juliet claims, sitting on the edge of my bed.

I let out a heavy sigh. "You always dog me when we go out."

"I do not," Juliet counters defensively.

My brow lifts as my head tilts slightly. "Seriously?"

"What?" Juliet replies, standing up, placing her hand on her hip.

I don't comment, allowing the unspoken truth to linger in the air. Knowing Juliet, I continue to stare her down, waiting for her to break.

"I don't know why you continue to put yourself in these kinds of situations," my inner voice states.

I mentally roll my eyes as if it'll get it to stop talking.

Unable to take the silence, Juliet finally admits, "It's not my fault that I end up finding a cute guy to hook up with when I'm out and you don't. You need to be more open to the option for yourself and you wouldn't be so mad at me about it."

The corner of my mouth ticks up for a few brief moments, pleased at Juliet's unprompted admittance about her promiscuous habits. It's been seven years, ever since we met in college and Juliet got us fake IDs, that I have played the role of guardian. There were other friends who joined us, but they too got drunk, left without saying a word, stranding Juliet and me on many occasions. Frustrated by the abandonment, I vowed to never let a girl go out by herself after an incident that happened just off-campus our first year.

"You need to be less open," I snicker.

Her eyes narrow. "How long has it been since Owen broke things off with you?"

I let out a sigh as I bite my lip. Juliet doesn't know the truth about what happened between Owen and me. Not one person knows. She's not wrong with calling me out. Since then, I've been avoiding men as much as possible for many months.

"Juliet," I huff.

"We don't go out as often as we used to," she whines.

I lift a brow.

"You moved away for so long, and even with us living together now, we barely go out," she adds with the tone of a toddler who's about to have a tantrum.

I don't reply, knowing that she'll eventually act more like an adult, which is the only way to sway me.

"I just don't want to appear desperate," Juliet sighs, leaning against the door frame.

I snort. "You're always desperate."

"She is way too desperate...it's sad," my inner voice cackles. "The very epitome of insanity...doing the same thing over and over again expecting a different result."

"It's not my fault that I'm twenty-eight and haven't found the right guy yet."

"Have you considered that your choice in men is the problem?" I ask snidely.

"Like you've done well in that department," Juliet quips back with sass.

My jaw tightens as I contemplate my response. "I'm picky," I claim with half-truth.

"Too picky," Juliet counters.

My shoulders bounce. "At least I can count the number of men I've slept with on one hand with another to spare."

"Ouch," Juliet replies with mock hurt feelings. "At least I'm figuring out what I prefer."

Her response makes me laugh. "I know what I prefer. I just don't need as many men to figure it out."

"They're fun, but not one of them has lasted long to satisfy my needs," Juliet sighs. "And, I'm not just talking about sexually."

"What about that one guy you hooked up with a few times? Tim…John…Jack—"

"Jake?" she scoffs. "Seriously, you bring up him?"

"Weren't you two an item for a while?" I goad.

"Don't," Juliet warns, holding up her hand in warning.

Though she always denies it, she was dating the guy for some time. How do I know? Aside from being her roommate, and the only person who goes out with her to the three different bars she likes to frequent, I had several nights of being stuck hanging out with Jake's friend.

"Wasn't he more open to exploration?" I inquire, biting back a snicker.

Juliet lets out a heavy exhale and rolls her eyes to avoid the topic further. We both know the truth behind that relationship. Things were going good between her and him—at least it seemed like it for a good four months until things abruptly ended.

"Most men are not willing to explore being pegged," I remind.

"They think it takes away their masculinity and makes them gay. You can't expect a man to be willing to have his ass penetrated."

"If any man is not willing to be pegged, yet expects my ass to be open for—"

"Please don't," I request, holding up my hand. "I don't need, nor want, details or the visual."

"They don't like it when you surprise them with a finger," Juliet laughs.

"Ew!" I chuck a pillow at her. "I don't want to hear that shit!"

"You brought it up," Juliet says, brushing it off with a shrug after dodging my weapon.

"Can we just stay in?" I beg. "It's snowing."

She glances out the window. "It's only flurrying. Besides, snow never kept us out of a bar before."

"They're calling for at least a foot," I say, hoping she'll change her mind. "And, I'm dressed for staying in."

"You've been dressed like that since this morning."

My shoulders bounce. "It's not my fault that I work from home and can wear whatever I want."

Juliet glances out the window. "It's barely started. We've got time for food and then—"

"Please?" I ask dramatically with clasped hands.

"There's a band tonight," she adds. "And, my lady needs tending to."

"You've got at least six different BOBs to assist with that," I remind.

"I need more than just BOB and his friends," Juliet claims.

My eyes roll though I understand the feeling. It's been a while since my relationship with Owen, let alone had a man inside my panties. Even though I have the same itch, that doesn't mean I'll be opening my legs for any man tonight. A girl needs to set some boundaries for herself and stick to them.

"Two feet," I remind.

"One foot," she counters.

"It could be two," I challenge. "Anytime New York has gotten a snowstorm this early in the season, there's more snow than they anticipate."

"So?"

"So, it might be a better idea to just booty call one of your—
"

Juliet takes in a long, deep, dramatic gasp.

My eyes dart to the ceiling for a moment. "You have no one you can—-"

Her hand darts up, signaling for me to stop. "How dare you?"

"How dare I?" I scoff with a snicker. "Please, bitch."

Juliet pouts. "I need me something new."

"Then...let's go to the toy store."

"Nope." She wags her finger at me. "I need the real deal."

My leg bounces as I contemplate how this discussion will continue until I cave and agree to go. She's right, we haven't been out in a while. I've avoided it as much as possible because of knowing where she wants to go and how it'll all unfold. I wait a few more seconds, deliberately enjoying the agony on Juliet's face as she silently pleas with me.

"Fine," I groan, closing my laptop.

"Yay!" Her hands dart above her head before she rushes over to hug me. "Thank you. Thank you. Thank you. Thank you!" Her lips contact my cheek several times.

I push her off of me as I attempt to rise from my bed. "The moment you find the one, please, for the love of God, get him and yourself out of the bar and to his place. I want to make it back here in one piece."

"Done," Juliet agrees.

An hour later, after showering and primping, Juliet is finally ready to find her meat stick for the night. I was ready twenty minutes ago—and that was taking my time.

Juliet beams as we step out of the cab and onto the sidewalk that's covered with a thin blanket of flurries. I scowl at the bite of the air, tightening my fingers around my jacket.

"Where's your coat?" I ask.

"Don't need it."

"I'm not taking care of your ass if—"

"I'll be fine," Juliet claims, jumping up and down to stay warm. "I just need a drink and I'll be good."

"I'm going to need more than a drink," I mumble, following her into the bar.

I continue to complain under my breath, stopping when I collide with her. She decided she needed a long pause just beyond the entrance to take in the crowd.

"Don't crowd me," Juliet whines.

"Don't stop halfway into the place," I quip.

Juliet turns sharply on her heels to face me. "I need you to be perky and happy tonight, okay?"

I offer a fake smile. "Sure."

"I mean it," she says with a hand on her hip.

"So do I," I lie through a clenched jaw.

I pray to God that this is the last night I'll ever have to babysit Juliet, assuring him or her, whichever God may be, that I'll do anything if Juliet would find her one true love tonight and relieve me of this insanity. I tolerate the girl more than most, but there's a girl code between single roommates.

"Hey," some creepy guy says walking up to us.

"Not interested," Juliet returns as she juts her chin in the opposite direction and walks away.

I avoid making eye contact with the guy and quickly follow her.

Juliet takes a table near the back right corner which is the area she prefers to sit whenever we come to The Smoked Goat.

She tries other places to hunt, but she's seemed to have the most success with finding a hookup, and a potential temporary boyfriend, at this particular location. Plus, Juliet likes the drama that surrounds the place. She gets noticed by guys we've seen before and others we haven't. Juliet likes the attention and the reputation she's built for herself. Stories have been known to circulate.

She sits in the corner seat with her back to the wall and peers out across the entire room with obvious excitement.

"Tone it down," I command.

"What?"

"You're an obvious beckon with flashing lights saying *I want to get fucked tonight*," I declare lowly. "Lock that shit up or else you'll attract all of the creepers."

"Right," Juliet replies, adjusting herself while pulling her v-neck shirt lower to expose more cleavage. She grabs the small drink menu in front of her from the table. "What should I have? Hmm…."

"A shot of common sense followed by a shot of I'm bored and want to go home," I answer.

"Boring," Juliet says in a sing-song voice. Her eyes stay engaged with the document in her hands.

I look around the bar after hanging my coat on the closest wall hook. There are some good-looking men tonight, but many already seem preoccupied by women or other men. There are a few I recognize from when we've been hunting here before, but I quickly shift my gaze to avoid eye contact with them.

We order drinks, and as they arrive, two guys approach us. I glance away as Juliet lets out a heavy sigh.

"Hey, girls," the shorter one greets, wiggling his eyebrows.

"Hi, Jake," Juliet replies with an unimpressed tone.

I could swear that Jake looks a bit different from the last time we saw him. I never got the details from Juliet as to why it all ended. Based on our conversation earlier, I'd have to assume it was a pegging issue.

Juliet has always been adventurous in the bedroom. Let me clarify. Juliet enjoys pushing a guy's boundaries in the bedroom more so than her willingness to partake in such activities. I think she's more curious than she'd like to admit, but she's not willing to do it if a guy isn't willing to let her do it to him first.

"What are you two up to tonight?" Jake continues, ignoring Juliet's brush-off.

"Not you," Juliet quips.

Jake laughs. "You liked it all those times before."

"I was drunk each time," Juliet counters. "I don't remember much…other than disappointment."

Jake's friend hovers close by, pretending not to notice our friends' conversation. He seems just as bored to be here like me.

Jake frowns with contention. "Well, I remember you screaming my name and I don't mind reminding you if—"

Juliet's hand darts up in his face. "Not interested." She takes a sip of her drink and stands up, righting her clothes before moving toward someone who's caught her eye.

"Not interested," I inform when Jake looks at me.

"You know she liked it more than she wants to admit," Jake claims.

"Wouldn't know," I sigh. "I wasn't there."

"You could be next time," Jake offers, trying to be slick.

I laugh. "Not even in your dreams."

"Leave her alone, Jake," his friend states, stepping between us.

"I saw her first, Wes," Jake claims.

I've known Wes' name since we first met, but I purposefully pretend that I don't remember it each time.

"Neither of you have a chance," I quip. "I suggest you move along."

Jake doesn't budge. "She'll be back."

Wes rolls his eyes.

"Of course she will," I return. "She came with me."

"How many times has she *come* with you?" Jake asks with a creepy grin.

I lean forward, offer a smile, and bit my lip. "I bet you'd like to really know that wouldn't you?"

Jake leans past Wes' arm, smiling from ear to ear.

"You enjoy torturing boys...particularly these two," my inner voice says with a laugh. "Oh, I do love these moments."

"How many times we've kissed...humped...and ate each other out," I say, baiting Jake more.

Wes snorts as he takes a sip of his drink, dribbling a little onto his shirt.

"Good one," my inner voice muses. "You got the cute player to fumble."

Jake's head bobs, eager for the juicy details.

I shift in my seat and lick my lips. "How many times I was able to satisfy her beyond your imagination and beyond your ability."

"I satisfied her," Jake claims.

"If you did such a great job, why aren't you two still fucking?" I lift my beer bottle and stick out my tongue, touching the rim right before taking a sip.

"She has a point," Wes interjects with a grunt.

I laugh at how I'm roasting Jake and have a witness to it. "You're an idiot if you believe anything has ever happened between my friend and me, and even if it did, you're more of an idiot to think I'd tell you."

"I could fuck you both so good that—"

Wes grabs Jake by the collar and yanks him away from me, placing himself between us.

"What the fuck, man?" Jake asks.

Wes sticks out his chest a little more and takes a step toward him.

"Alright," Jake replies, holding his hands up. "Alright. Alright. She's yours. I got you."

"I'm not his," I shout at Jake as he walks away. I take a gulp of my beer. "I'm not impressed."

"I wasn't trying to impress you."

"Methinks you're trying to impress him yet again," my inner voice states.

"Right," I laugh with a mocking tone. "This isn't the first time."

"What's that supposed to mean?" Wes replies.

"Every time your friend and you see my friend and me, you both try to hit on us."

"She did put out," Wes reminds. "You can't blame the guy if he's pussy whipped."

I snort, taking in a small bit of my beer into my nose which immediately starts to burn. Ducking out of the way, I search for a napkin while keeping my face covered.

"Here," Wes offers.

"Thanks," I say, begrudgingly taking it. I clean myself the best that I can without looking any more like a fool.

"You okay?" he asks.

I nod, taking another sip as I look away.

"Oh no. What's happening?" my inner voice asks.

"Well, at least we're even."

"Not funny," I reply, wiping my nose a final time.

"So…why do you come out if you're going to be grumpy every time?"

My brow lifts as I look back at Wes. "I'm not grumpy."

"You might as well be wearing a sign that says—"

"Closed for business? Need not apply?" I reply sharply.

Wes chuckles. "No." He thinks for a second. "I would have said *stick up ass and unwilling to remove it.*"

"I don't have a stick up my ass," I counter.

Wes leans back as if to check. He doesn't comment, but his expression disagrees.

"Oh, girl, he just checked out your ass again. He so wants you," my inner voice says excitedly.

"Your weak attempts of flirting aren't working," I inform.

"Who says I'm flirting?" He takes a sip of his beer.

"Look at his luscious lips wrapped around that bottle. That could be us," sighs my inner voice.

"You're still here…at my table," I remind.

"You're flirting with him, too," my inner voice balks.

Wes purses his lips and looks around the room. "It is a good spot." He takes another sip. "Great view of eighty percent of all the asses in here."

"Pig."

Wes leans close to my ear—a little too close. "I didn't mean the female rear-ends."

"Right."

"Most of the guys here are dicks," he adds, finally pulling away.

"I'd say all of them."

"I'm not a dick," Wes claims.

"Says the player," I counter with a snicker.

"He may be a player, but you and I know we both want to tap that," my inner voice coos. "God. He always smells good, too."

"Who says I'm a player?"

My shoulders bounce. "Word gets around."

"You should hear the rumors about your friend."

I bite back a smile. "It's her reputation, not mine."

"So. Who says I'm a—"

"Simone!" Juliet shrieks with excitement, suddenly at my side. "Meet Leonardo. Isn't he handsome?"

"Yes," I agree, leaning away from Juliet's intrusion on my

personal space. My shoulder bumps into Wes, but he doesn't move.

"Um, excuse me," Juliet says, looking at Wes.

He doesn't say anything, nor does he move.

"I need some alone time with my girl," Juliet demands, flicking her hand at Wes to shoo.

Wes looks at me and then at Leonardo before walking away by a mere ten feet.

"Anyway," Juliet huffs. "What was I saying? Right. Simone, this is Leonardo. Leonardo, this is Simone."

"Hello, beautiful Simone," Leonardo greets with an accent, he takes my hand and kisses it. "It is my pleasure to meet you."

"He's Italian!" Juliet says excitedly.

"Nice to meet you," I reply, pulling my hand from his grip.

"We're going to dance," Juliet announces. She pulls him toward the open space where a few other people are dancing. I let out a sigh, thankful that I'm not going to have to engage in polite conversation with a stranger.

For the next hour, when I'm not glancing around the bar, finding Wes staring at me each time, I watch Juliet and Leonardo grinding on each other. My instinct is to chug more of my beer and look away, but I almost choke each time as the sickening spectacle flashes in my head.

"Here," a voice to my left says.

A man's hand extends with a glass of clear liquid.

I look up to find Wes. "What's this?"

"Water," he claims. "It'll be easier and less likely to make you want to vomit."

"Why would I—"

Wes points toward Juliet and Leonardo. "It is scary. I think it's almost as bad as when she and Jake were dating."

I curl my lips in, trying to hide my amusement. My hand reaches for the glass, but then I push it toward him. "I'm good."

"Drink it," he insists.

"I'm good with my beer."

"Simone—"

"I don't want it," I say.

I usually do have water at some point in the night, but I've been nursing the same bottle of beer since we arrived.

"It's only water."

I pick it up, sniff it, and then slide it back toward him.

"Seriously?" he scoffs.

"Seriously," I reply. "For all I know, you put a date-rape drug in there."

"But would we honestly mind if he took advantage of us?" my inner voice asks.

Wes lets out a huff. "You know me."

"Not really," I reply.

"How many times have we seen each other?"

"Could still be drugged."

"You didn't seem to mind when we first met," he reminds. "And, several other times when our friends were dating."

"It's still creepy."

"How?" he snorts. "How is this time any different?"

I shrug. "I watched you buy those other ones."

"Seriously?" he replies with a grunt.

"How am I supposed to know you aren't a serial killer or rapist? You're working on not appearing creepy to offer me a drink which then leads to suspicion that you are, in fact, trying to—"

"You watch too many violent shows," Wes interjects.

"I don't watch much tv. Besides, I'm merely realistic and—"

"Crazy," Wes chuckles. He takes the glass and takes a sip. "There. If I was drugging you, then I've obviously drugged myself, too."

I peer down at the glass. "One, you sipped it, which wouldn't be enough for a man your size. And, two, ew! I'm not drinking it now."

"Germaphobe?" he laughs as he gulps half of the glass. Wes slams it down on the table, which makes it spill a little, and pushes it toward me. "There. Happy?"

"No."

Suddenly, the table rocks and I find Juliet and Leonardo laughing and leaning on it. Wes catches the glass of water, blocking it from spilling on either of us.

"We're going," Juliet announces.

"Thank the lord!" my inner voice huffs. "We're finally free from this night. Can we take the hottie to go though, please? It's been way too long without any action. Shit. Look at how you keep talking to him. You need to get laid or else it's just you and me forever."

Juliet's eyes scan Wes from head to toe. "Why are you bothering her?"

"Someone needs to keep an eye on her while you're—"

Juliet darts her hand in front of Wes' face. "It was rhetoric."

"Rhetorical," Wes corrects.

I literally almost snot on myself but recover with a cough.

"Did I ask you?" Juliet jabs with her hand on her hip.

"Is that one rhetoric?" Wes replies with a straight face.

My lips curl inward and I press down on them to prevent a smile.

"Damn, I forgot how funny he is," my inner voice muses. "Why can't you just have one night with him? Please!"

Juliet isn't dumb, but she doesn't use her brain as regularly as she could and should. If she did, Juliet would actually find a decent guy rather than all the assholes she attracts.

"Ew," Juliet gasps.

I quickly check my face, whipping my hand as nonchalantly as possible.

Thankfully, Juliet's disgust is at Wes.

"Why are you even here?" Juliet returns snidely.

"We're back at this again?" Wes replies with a smile, looking at me as if he's waiting for me to react.

My head sways ever so slightly, hoping he doesn't push that topic again.

"Weren't you going?" Wes asks.

"Not that it's any of your business, but we are," Juliet confirms. "Come on, Simone."

I catch a sly smile creep on Leonardo's face.

"I'm not going with you two," I reply with a chuckle, pulling my arm away from Juliet.

"You can't be seriously thinking about staying with him?" Juliet gestures with her head toward Wes.

"I'm right here," Wes quips.

I let out a sigh. "I'm not going with him."

"Good," Juliet replies, narrowing her eyes at Wes. "You're too good for him."

"You've got everything?" I ask Juliet, hoping to redirect her attention.

"Yeah," she says with a smile.

"I'm serious."

"Me, too," Juliet replies. "I'm good. You're relieved of duty, mom."

"Text me."

"I will," Juliet says with a wave of her hand in the air as she walks away with Leonardo in tow.

"She never texts," my inner voice reminds. "You'll think she's been ditched in a dark ally until she suddenly staggers through the door."

"You trust her to—"

"Don't!" I chide. I chance a glance at Wes. "Just, don't."

"Is it just me, or did something about that guy bug you?"

My brow lifts. "Asks the guy who offers me a drink that may be drugged."

Wes rolls his eyes. "What now?"

"I'm going home."

Wes steps back and offers me my jacket.

"Alone," I state.

"I was just assisting you," Wes claims.

I study him for a moment. With not a single sign of him appearing to be drugged or anything other than the Wes I know, I snatch the half glass of water and chug the rest of it.

Slamming the glass on the table, I shout, "There! Happy?"

"Just get home safe and then I'll be happy."

"Aww," I sigh. "Player has a heart."

"He's got a cock too if you'd just be willing to use it like you need," *my inner voice states.*

BUY Snowed In With Him NOW to finish the story

ABOUT THE AUTHOR

Martha Sweeney is a Best-Selling author who writes in a variety of genres: romance, suspense, thriller, coloring books, romantic comedy, and science fiction. She strives to push herself as a storyteller with each new tale and hopes to push her readers outside of their comfort zone whether it be genre or the stories themselves.

With a B.S. in Psychology, Martha utilizes her knowledge of human and animal behavior successfully in the business world and in her writing to present realistic characters and situations. She's been creative since she was little, always drawing, coloring or making crafts, so her venture into being an author was a natural transition.

Connect with Martha:
www.marthasweeney.com
Newsletter Signup: http://eepurl.com/dGAuQD

9 798227 552945